Carousel
Round and Round

Carousel Round

and Round by Kay Chorao

Clarion Books/New York

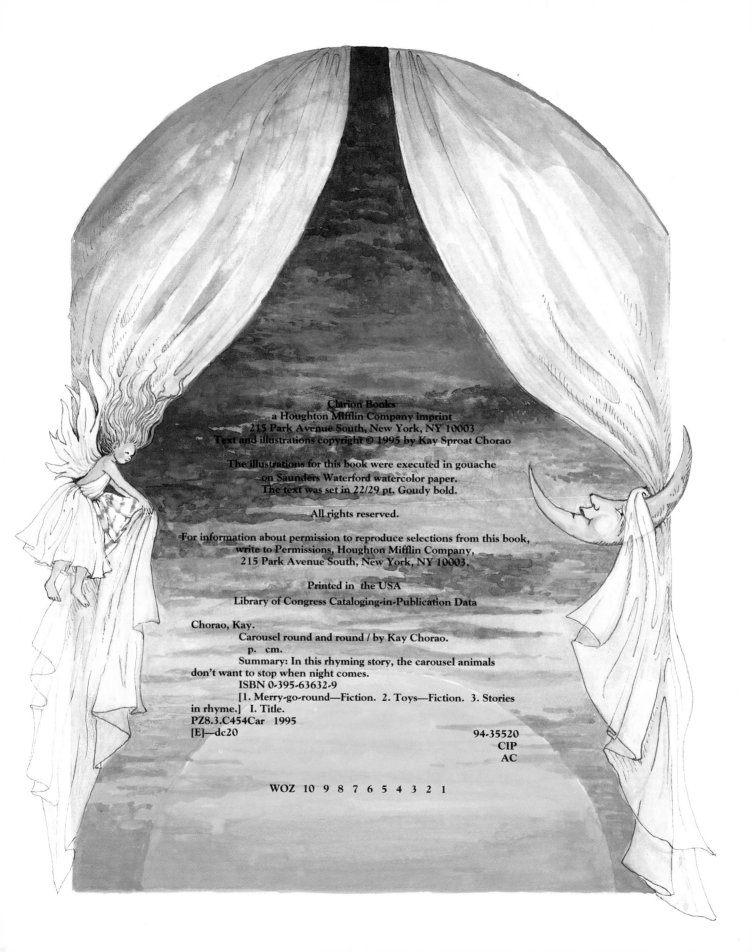

Clarion Books
a Houghton Mifflin Company imprint
215 Park Avenue South, New York, NY 10003
Text and illustrations copyright © 1995 by Kay Sproat Chorao

The illustrations for this book were executed in gouache
on Saunders Waterford watercolor paper.
The text was set in 22/29 pt. Goudy bold.

Printed in the USA

Library of Congress Cataloging-in-Publication Data

Chorao, Kay.
        Carousel round and round / by Kay Chorao.
            p.   cm.
        Summary: In this rhyming story, the carousel animals
don't want to stop when night comes.
        ISBN 0-395-63632-9
        [1. Merry-go-round—Fiction. 2. Toys—Fiction. 3. Stories
in rhyme.] I. Title.
PZ8.3.C454Car 1995
[E]—dc20   94-35520
                                                               CIP
                                                               AC

WOZ 10 9 8 7 6 5 4 3 2 1

For Ernesto

(with special thanks
to Michael Murphy and his parents)

The sun was going down.
The moon was coming up.
And the carousel circled
round and round.

Round and round,
up and down.
The animals circled
round and round.

Slower and slower the carousel moved.
The moon rose orange in the dusk-blue sky.
The carousel lion narrowed one eye.

Slower and slower the carousel moved.
The stars glittered bright,
little pinpoints of light.
The carousel pig said, "It's too early for night."

11

Slower and slower
the carousel moved.
The carousel horse,
without a sound
lifted his hooves
and pawed the ground.

Slower and slower
the carousel moved.
"Yes, it's too early to stop,"
said the carousel swan.
But she lifted her head
and made a swan-yawn.

Slower and slower the carousel moved.
Softer and softer the carousel sound

of carousel music, round and round.
Until at last the carousel stopped.

Under the moon
and the bright sprinkled stars
the animals stepped
from their carousel perch.

18

They pushed and shoved
and shoved and pushed,
but the only move
was a carousel lurch.

19

"I wanted more," said Lion to Horse.
"I wanted more, too," said Pig to Swan.
"Shhhhh," said Horse, "I hear a sound."

Then Horse bent down and put his ear to the ground.

21

"The *giant*, the *giant*," warned the horse.
"Dear me, dear me," mumbled the pig.
"Find your places," ordered the lion.
"And keep very still," hissed the swan.

No sooner had each hopped back to his place,
than giant hands sprang from outer space.
The hands grabbed hold of the carousel.
They lifted it high in the starry night.
The lion and horse, the pig and swan
kept very still and held on tight.

Would they slip? Would they crash?
Would they fall? Would they smash?
But the brave little animals held on tight.
They kept very still in the starry night.

Then the giant clicked and clacked a key.
And music rose. Hear! Could it be?
The carousel began to turn
round and round, up and down.
The carousel circled
round and round.

Then the giant went back to his giant bed
and quietly settled his giant head.

But under the stars
and the moon that night
the carousel circled
round and round.

The carousel circled round and round.